Kingdom Lessons for Life

Christian Fables

on

Faith and Trust

Christy Ojikutu

Book 1 of the Christian Fable Series

for Children and Families

Kingdom Lessons for Life
Christian Fables on Faith and Trust

Copyright© 2025 by Christy Ojikutu

All rights reserved.

Unless otherwise noted, Scripture quotations are taken from the New King James Version®.Copyright © 1982 by Thomas Nelson. Used by permission. All rights reserved

Published by WhollyBooks
Whollybooks.com

ISBN 978-1-968787-24-0 (pbk)
ISBN 978-1-968787-25-7 (eBook)
Printed in the United States of America

Table of Contents

About This Series

The *Kingdom Lessons for Life* series is a collection of Christian fables designed to teach children–and families–important spiritual lessons through engaging, relatable stories. Each book in the series focuses on a different aspect of faith, character, and Godly wisdom, encouraging young readers to grow in trust, obedience, and love for God.

Through imaginative stories, reflection questions, Scripture verses, and morals of stories, children are invited to see faith in action and learn that God's guidance is present in everyday life. The series helps lay a foundation for a lifetime of spiritual growth, resilience, and Kingdom-minded living.

Books in the Series Include:

1. Kingdom Lessons for Life: Christian Fables on Faith and Trust

2. Kingdom Lessons for Life: Christian Fables on Courage and Strength

3. Kingdom Lessons for Life: Christian Fables on Humility and Pride

4. Kingdom Lessons for Life: Christian Fables on Kindness and Compassion

(More volumes are coming, each designed to nurture faith, character, and spiritual growth in young readers and families!)

Look for the *Kingdom Lessons for Life* series label on each title to easily identify books in this collection.

Preface

Welcome to *Kingdom Lessons for Life: Christian Fables on Faith and Trust*. This book was written with a simple goal: to help children—and families—learn how to trust God in everyday life. Through short and meaningful stories, you will experience the challenges, joys, and lessons that come when faith meets real-life situations.

These fables are more than just stories; they are invitations to reflect, pray, and grow. Each fable will encourage children to notice God at work in their lives, even when life is uncertain, ultimately helping them to understand that trust in God brings peace, courage, and wisdom.

Whether you are reading alone, reading together at bedtime, or discussing the reflection questions with your family, these stories are designed to spark conversations, inspire hearts, and build a foundation of faith that lasts a lifetime.

Acknowledgments

I would like to express my deepest gratitude to God, whose wisdom, enlightenment, and knowledge made this series possible. Thank you to my family, whose encouragement, and support nurtured the writing of these stories. Additionally, I would like to appreciate the mentors, teachers, and friends who inspire faith-filled living and help sow seeds of trust in young hearts every day.

To the children who will read these fables: thank you for reminding us how to see life with wonder and curiosity and faith. Your joy and trust remind us why these stories matter.

Dedication

For children—the dreamers, questioners, and explorers! May your hearts always trust God's timing and care.

For courageous parents, guardians, and mentors! May you foster faith, courage, and hope in every story you share.

Introduction

Life is full of moments that challenge our trust in big and small ways. Children face challenges at school, with friends, and at home just as adults face uncertainty with their work, relationships, and personal goals. In these moments, learning to trust God can lead to peace and strength.

Kingdom Lessons for Life gives young minds a chance to see faith in action. Each of the fables is a light-hearted story to gently remind children to see God at work. From the story on the sparrow who forgot to sing to the story on the fireflies who compare themselves to the stars, and other stories, children are reminded that God's timing, wisdom, and care are always present—even when it is not obvious.

Each fable comes along with a story moral, reflection questions, a verse of Scripture that will encourage children to think, pray, and trust. By reading these stories, children will enjoy every adventure and learn valuable lessons about humility, patience, courage, and hope. My prayer is that when you and your children read these stories, you will see that faith is not just something learned, it is something to be lived out every day.

1

The Sparrow Who Forgot to Sing
(Resting in God's Care)

In a still and quiet corner of the forest, there lived a small sparrow named Simeon. Each morning, just before the sun began to warm the treetops, Simeon would fly to the highest branch of his favorite tree and sing a little song—a song that was full of hope and quiet confidence. It wasn't loud or impressive—but to Simeon, it meant the world. It was his way of saying, "God will take care of me today."

But one morning felt different.

The sky above loomed with thick, gray clouds and the wind moved stiffly through the trees, sighing as though it knew something was coming. The river that usually babbled below now churned with restless energy. Simeon perched on his branch, uneasy. There was a tight knot forming in his chest.

"What if it a storm comes and I can't find food?" he thought anxiously. *"What if it rains for days? What if I get cold or wet or worse... hungry and with no way to fix it?"*

So instead of singing like he always did, Simeon took off, darting from branch to branch in a frenzy, eyes flitting and heart racing. He searched frantically for food, trying to stay out of a storm that had not even started. His usual peace and calm had vanished.

He was too focused on surviving to notice a bluebird close by offering him a tasty, juicy worm, or a subtle wind blowing him toward a bush heavy with ripe, delicious berries.

By the time the sun began to disappear from view in the evening, no storm had come, but Simeon was completely drained. He wings ached from flying all day. His tummy was empty, and his heart felt even heavier than his body.

When he reached his nest, he crawled in and breathed a very deep sigh. On a few branches above him was a robin named Rosanna—older, wiser, and always kind. She quietly looked at him for a moment before speaking.

Softly, she said, "Simeon...I didn't hear you sing this morning! Are you alright?" He looked up at her, and with a voice barely more than a whisper, he admitted, "I was afraid. I thought I had to figure it all out by myself."

Rosanna nodded, her expression warm. "Oh, sweet Simeon... singing doesn't mean the storm won't come. It just reminds your heart of who holds the storm. You don't sing because you have it all together; you sing because God does."

The next morning, the clouds were still hanging low, the wind had not completely settled. But Simeon got up anyway. He took his place on his favorite branch, fluffed his feathers up and let out a soft, shaky note. Then another. And another. It was not his strongest song, but it was filled with something more important – faith.

And as the very last note drifted through the air, a single drop of rain slid off a leaf and landed just below him--right next to a wiggling worm.

Moral of the Story:

Even when the future feels uncertain, choosing to trust God opens the door to peace and unexpected provision.

Scripture Verse:

"Look at the birds of the air, for they neither sow nor reap nor gather into barns; yet your heavenly Father feeds them. Are you not of more value than they?" — Matthew 6:26

Reflection Questions:

1. Have you ever found yourself worrying so much that your distress drowned out your trust in God? What helped to restore your heart to peace?

2. What small act of trust can you do today, such as Simeon's song?

3. How does remembering your value to God change the way you face uncertainty or fear?

2
The Ant Who Waited for Rain
(Learning Patience in God's Timing)

Just beyond the edge of the field, amidst soil cracked and crumbly from the sun, lived a small ant named Amos. Amos was not particularly strong or fast, but he was known in the colony for being thoughtful. He did not rush; he listened and always tried to do the right thing, even when it didn't make sense to others.

One summer, the rains stopped coming.

Days and days of sunshine slowly baked the earth, leaving the ground cracked and dry like spider webs. The leaves turned brown and drooped off the trees. The grass became dull. Food was hard to find and the other ants in the colony began to grow anxious.

"We need to leave!" said one of the ants. "What are we doing here waiting and hoping for rain to come? We need to dig deeper, search farther, do something!"

But Amos would not leave.

He sat in the same dried-up place, where the brook once trickled through the ground near the rocks. Every morning, he came there, he sat still, and he waited.

"Why do you keep coming back to that dry patch?" said a frustrated ant. "There is no water, no food, and no point."

Amos looked up calmly. "Because this is where the water always came. I believe it'll come again. I just don't know when."

The other ant shook his head and marched off to the hills in search for food.

Days went by. The air was hotter and the ground drier. Every morning Amos continued to return to the same, quiet place. He did not talk much. He just waited. Patiently. Hopeful. Calm and steady, even when the sky stayed dry..

Then, one evening, just as the sun began to drop below the trees, a cool breeze blew across the field. Clouds rolled in quietly and a single drop of rain hit Amos on the back. Then another. And then another.

Before long, the dry ground turned soft. The dry brook by the rocks shimmered with water again.

The ants that had gone up the hills rushed back, tired and worn out. When they made it back, they found Amos by the newly filled brook, drinking slowly, and smiling quietly.

"You stayed!" said an ant in surprise.

"I trusted," said Amos. "Sometimes faith means staying still when everything around you says to run."

Moral of the story:

Patience isn't doing nothing; it's holding on to hope when everything else says to give up.

Scripture verse:

"But those who wait on the Lord shall renew their strength; they shall mount up with wings like eagles, they shall run and not be weary, they shall walk and not faint." — Isaiah 40:31

Reflection Questions:

1. Have you ever felt like giving up because circumstance around did not change quickly enough? What helped you hold on?

2. What does it mean for you to "wait on the Lord" in your life right now?

3. How can waiting with faith and patience strengthen your trust in God's timing?

3

The Brave Little Seed
(Trusting God With Small Beginnings)

Deep in a farmer's sack, buried in with a dozen other seeds, rested a little seed named Silas. He was small—smaller than most of the others and quieter too; but he had big dreams. He had heard the other seeds talk about what it meant to grow, to push through the soil, and to become something more than a shell.

One morning, the farmer came to the field. He gently opened his bag of seeds, scattered them in the soil, and just like that, some seeds rolled along soft earth, while others rolled into the shade. Silas, however, tumbled into a hole that felt...dark.

Very dark.

Silas laid there, for a long while, cold, buried, not even sure of his surroundings. The silence of being underground was heavy, and doubt crept in.

Why did the farmer leave me here? he wondered. I'm alone. I can barely breathe. Maybe I wasn't meant to grow at all.

Time passed. Rain fell. The soil began to shift. Something very deep inside Silas began to stir. It was not loud. It was not obvious. It was a gentle nudge, a soft whisper saying, Push. Stretch. Keep going.

It took everything that was left in him to trust that whisper. He began to push upward. He did not know where he was headed. There was no way of seeing the surface. But he still believed, somewhere deep down, that there was light waiting for him.

It took days.

And then, one morning, his little green tip broke through the soil. Sunlight kissed his leaves. Warmth embraced him. Silas was not just a seed, he was beginning to grow.

From the edge of the field, the farmer smiled. He had not forgotten about Silas. He knew exactly where he'd planted him. And he knew exactly what was about to happen.

Moral of the Story:

Sometimes growth feels like darkness, but God is as work beneath the surface.

Trust the process.

Scripture Verse:

"Most assuredly, I say to you, unless a grain of wheat falls into the ground and dies, it remains alone; but if it dies, it produces much grain." — John 12:24

Reflection Questions:

1. Have you ever felt "buried" in a hard situation? What helped you to keep going, when you couldn't see the outcome?

2. What is one area of your life where God may be growing something—just beneath the surface?

3. How can you remind yourself to trust God's unseen work, even when the results take time to appear?

4

The Cloud That Wouldn't Move
(Letting God Lead)

In the wide sky above the valley, there floated a fluffy little cloud named Clary. Clary was a soft, billowy little thing—fluffier than most clouds, and she was always curious where the wind would carry her.

Clary had a favorite thing: drifting. She loved floating gently through the forests and fields, peeking down at the rivers, listening to the swoosh of the trees, and playing tag with the birds. The wind would gently nudge her this way and that, and on she would glide through the sky with glee.

But one morning, something unusual happened

Clary woke up, just like any other time, to a nudge from the wind, but when she tried to move—nothing happened. It was as if some invisible hands were gently holding her in placed. She puffed and tugged and twisted… to no avail. She was still just hovering there, stuck.

"What's wrong with me?" she puffed. "Why am I not moving?"

A flock of geese flew by and called: "Come on, Cloud! Aren't you going to glide today?"

Clary called back, "I want to! But I can't. I'm stuck!"

The geese shrugged and disappeared into the horizon, while Clary sank further down in the sky, her edges droopy with frustration. She didn't like to sit still, she didn't like to wait, but most importantly she didn't like not knowing.

The hours passed, the sun crept across the sky. Below, the ground appeared parched and dry, the trees looked weary. A small village nestled in the valley below sat perfectly still—residents moving in the heat, slowly.

Then, just as time faded into evening, Clary felt something stir deep inside. She didn't know how she knew—it wasn't a voice and it wasn't a sign—but something whispered, Now.

This time she didn't need the wind. She began to move on her own, just a little. As she drifted forwards, she felt heavy—full of water that she hadn't even realized she was holding. And before long, the first drop of rain fell.

Then another. And another.

It poured softly across the valley—cooling the rooftops, soaking the gardens, filling empty wells. The people below tilted their heads in relief, dancing in the sprinkles, smiling in the rain.

Clary grinned.

She finally understood. She hadn't been stuck.

She had been sent – to stay, and wait, and to bring life at the exact moment it was needed most.

Moral of the Story

Sometimes God asks us to stay put, even when we don't understand why. Trusting Him means that we acknowledge His timing is better than ours.

Scripture Verse:

"The Lord went before them by day in a pillar of cloud to lead the way…" — Exodus 13:21

Reflection Questions:

1. Have you ever felt like you were stuck and not moving forward when you desperately wanted to? What do you think God may have been doing during that time of waiting?
2. Is there anything in your life right now that God may be asking you to wait on?
3. How do you practice trusting God when He doesn't provide you with all the answers?

5

The Shepherd and the Shadow
(Conquering Fear Through Trust in God)

On the edge of a peaceful meadow lived a young shepherd named Eli. He wasn't the strongest shepherd on the mountainside, but he had something better – he had a great love for his sheep. Every day, he led them out to graze in the green pastures, and to drink from the stream that wound its way gently through the valley. One evening, as the sun began to sink, Eli noticed something unusual in the sky. Not the usual onset of night, but a thick, dark shadow that stretched down upon the earth. It was moving slowly across the hills, blotting out the final bits of light. The sheep sensed it too. They huddled tightly together, bleating softly as their eyes widened in fear.

Eli swallowed hard. The shadow wasn't a storm cloud. It wasn't a flock of birds passing overhead. It was the shadow of the canyon — a dark, steep, cliffside crag that Eli had been too cautious to try to drive his sheep through before. But tonight, the grass was in the meadows was nearly gone, and the water was running low. He had hope; he'd heard other shepherds mention a lush field beyond the canyon—a place of lush, green pastures and clear streams. The trouble was to get there, he would have to walk through the shadowy pass of the canyon.

Eli took a deep breath and glanced quickly at his sheep. They always trusted him. They followed him everywhere. But tonight, standing at the mouth of the canyon, Eli felt smaller than ever – too small for the narrow path ahead. Then it came to him; his father said:

"Shadows only mean light is close by. Trust the One who holds both."

Eli carried those words inside his heart. He held his staff in one hand, prayed silently, and walked into the canyon.

At first, the sheep were hesitant but followed closely to him; they brushed against him, with their hooves clacking against the stony trail. The shadow grew darker as they marched deeper into the canyon. The wind moaned back and forth between the rock walls, and the darkness continued on without end. Still, he moved forward. Each step he took was a choice: fear… or trust.

Eventually, after what seemed like hours, a sliver of light appeared in the horizon. It grew larger with every step until

23

they stepped out of the canyon and into a wide, open field bathed in moonlight. The field was thick with soft grass. There was a rushing stream nearby that sparkled in the night. The sheep ran ahead and grazed on the thick grass.

Eli dropped to sit on a rock, and he felt a wave of relief wash over him. The shadow was real, but so was the Shepherd who had led him through it.

Moral of the Story

Fear is not an indication that God has left us. Even in dark uncertain places, His light is much closer than we think. It pushes back the fear and leads us forward with courage.

Scriptural Verse

"Yea, though I walk through the valley of the shadow of death, I will fear no evil; for You are with me; Your rod and Your staff, they comfort me." - Psalm 23:4

Reflection Questions

1. What "shadows" or fears have you felt recently?
2. How can you remind yourself that even when you don't see the way, God is walking beside you?
3. What is one brave act of faith you can take this week to trust God to walk you through?

6
The Candle in the Storm
(Faith During Trials)

In a small cottage on the edge of a village, there lived a single candle on a wooden shelf. Her name was Calla. Even though she was small, she loved being a candle and being a light in the darkness. As the family returned home each night, Calla would be lit, and her little light would fill the room with a soft glow.

And then one night, a storm came. Not just any storm. A raging storm that shook the windows, and howled through the cracks, and cast thick shadows across the walls. The power flickered and finally went out and was replaced with darkness so thick that it seemed to push against the walls.

"Quick! Light the candle!" someone whispered.

Calla felt the warmth of the matchstick at her wick, and in the very next moment, her tiny little flame sprang to life. She flickered a little unsteadily at first, swaying as the wind hissing through the shutters and swirled about the house.

"Steady," the grandmother whispered while cupping her hands to protect the flame, "We're going to need your light."

Calla wasn't so sure. The wind roared. The rain pounded even harder. The shadows grew, taller and stranger, twisting like restless shapes across the floor. "I'm too little for this!" Calla thought as she swayed and jiggled. "What if I go out? What if I can't possibly shine bright enough?"

And then Calla noticed all the faces gathered so closely, their eyes intently focused on her light. The family had circled together, holding hands and softly whispering prayers. And the moment her flame flickered it seemed someone whispered "Stay with us, little one."

And then, Calla realized something simple. It wasn't about being the brightest candle; it was about being the willing candle. A little candle can push away a lot of darkness. So, she burned, not perfectly, not without flickering here and there but she burned faithfully. All through the long stormy night, she burned.

And when morning came, the storm had passed, and sunlight flooded the windows, Calla's flame was gently blown out–not because darkness had overpowered her light–but because the light had returned.

Moral of the Story

Faith is not about the strongest light; it's about choosing to shine when the storm feels bigger than we are.

Scripture Verse

"You are the light of the world. A city set on a hill cannot be hidden." — Matthew 5:14

Reflection Questions

1. Have you ever felt too small or weak to make a difference? How might God choose to work through you regardless?
2. What "storm" are you facing that needs a little spark of faith?
3. Who around you might need your light right now– your encouragement, prayer, or kindness?

7

The Fox Who Followed His Own Path
(Disobedience vs Trust)

In a peaceful forest, where the tall grass swayed beside the bubbling, clear streams, lived a young fox named Felix with his family. Felix, being clever and curious, would dash off, always searching for new trails, hidden pathways, and secret places where no other fox would dare to go.

One morning, Felix's father said, "We are going to cross the meadow to the berry grove today. Stick close and follow my path. The grass is tall and snares are hidden in them... this is the only safe path to use."

Felix nodded but only half-listened. His mind was busy already and he was eyeing the neat trail off to the left, which looked shorter, smoother, and unworn; it was unexplored.

Once Felix and his family set off, he lingered back watching his father's worn trail and the nice, inviting little path him that beckoned. Why should I take the long way when I can find my own path? I am fast, I am smart, and I can get there before them. He glanced back to make sure no one was watching him. Without warning, Felix darted off in to the new path.

The grass swished around his paws, the dew on the air was fresh, and he thought, "See! much better than the boring trail."

But soon his path narrowed. Brambles snagged at his fur, and the ground was uneven. And then *snap*! Felix froze as he felt a thin rope tighten around his paw. Felix was in a hunter's snare.

Fear seeped into his chest, Felix pulled and twisted, but the more he struggled, the more the snare tightened. His heart was racing. He wished–oh, how he wished–he had stayed close to his father's feet.

In that moment, Felix heard the rustling. His father appeared, calm but firm. "Felix," he said softly while taking off the snare with his gentle paws, "the path I was taking was not to stop you from experiencing adventure, it was to keep you safe."

Felix hung his head in shame and guilt. "I thought I could do a better job."

His father smiled gently. "Next time, trust the one who can see danger before you can."

From that day forward, Felix would follow closely–not because he had to, but because he wanted to.

Moral of the Story

Obedience isn't about losing freedom; it's about trusting that God sees the danger we don't.

Scripture Verse

"Trust in the Lord with all your heart, and lean not on your own understanding; in all your ways acknowledge Him, and He shall direct your paths." - Proverbs 3:5-6

Reflection Questions

1. Have you ever followed your own path instead of God's leading? What was the result?
2. Why is it sometimes a struggle to trust God's path instead of your own?
3. What is one step of obedience you can take this week even when it seems harder than your own path?

8

The Broken Net
(Relying on God's Provision)

As daylight broke, the sun rose above the horizon, casting a glistening light on the surface of the water as Simon and his friends cast their nets into the lake. After fishing and trying all night with nothing to show for it, Simon whispered a little prayer: "Lord, let today be different."

Hours passed. The boat rocked gently in the calm waters, but the nets came up empty every time. The men were becoming frustrated. Fatigue settled over them like an invisible blanket. They were hungry and Simon started to wonder if God had forgotten them also.

As the afternoon passed, they saw Jesus walking along by the shoreline and he called out, "Throw your nets on the other side of the boat." This made no sense. They had just spent a long night fishing, and no one knew these waters better than Simon and his friends! But there was something about the sound of the His voice that stirred up hope in Simon's heart. They obeyed.

They nets sank into the water, and suddenly they jerked so intensely that Simon felt like he was going to be thrown overboard. Beneath the surface, fish were thrashing and glimmering — they caught more than they had ever caught at once; it was unbelievable! The men shouted in amazement as they strained together to haul the net in. It was strained to the breaking point, yet it somehow held.

The boat overflowed with so much fish that it nearly sank. Simon dropped to his knees, trembling before Jesus. "Lord, depart from me, for I am a sinful man."

But Jesus smiled, placed his hand on Simon's shoulder and said "Don't be afraid! From now on you will catch people instead of fish."

The overflowing nets were not just about provision; they were about calling. God was showing Simon that even when he felt defeated, the true work had only just begun.

Moral of the story

Even in the midst of troubles, God is still in control–and His plans are always greater than we can see. He can redeem any situation and turn it around for His purpose and our good.

Scripture Verse

"And we know that all things work together for good to those who love God, to those who are the called according to His purpose." - Romans 8:28

Reflection questions

1. Do you remember a time when it felt like your efforts were wasted, but God turned things around?

2. What does this story teach you about obedience, even when it does not make sense?

3. What is one area of your life where you need to trust God, even though things are not going as planned?

9

The Kite Who Feared the Wind
(Yielding to God's Strength)

Once upon a time, there was a small seaside village with a shed. Inside the shed, there was a bright red kite hanging on a nail. The kite had never been flown. Day after day, the wind called to the kite, whistling through the cracks in the walls, and saying, "Come and soar with me." But the kite was trembled.

"What if I tear? What if I fall? What if the wind is too strong?" it thought to itself.

One sunny afternoon the boy who owned the kite decided to take it to a vast open space. The breeze began to flow up through the tall grass around the kite and the wind began to tug on the frame of the kite and invite it to come fly with it. But still, the kite resisted and clung tightly to the boy's hand.

"I am afraid!" it cried silently, *"I not sure I can trust the wind to hold me."*

So, the boy knelt down close to the kite and spoke softly as if he could hear the kite's fears and said, "you were made to fly, not to sit in the shadows of a shed. But to rise, you must lean into the wind, not fight against it."

Bit by bit, the boy released his grip and the breeze began to lift the kite. At first the kite wobbled and dipped in the wind, but the stronger the wind got the more stable the kite became. What was once a fearful threat to the kite became the very force that carried it higher.

From up in the sky the kite began to see, and to feel, a beautiful world that it had never imagined—the waves, the hills. and the wide horizon. And, it also realized something powerful about its experience; the wind was never meant to break it but only to take it higher than it could go alone.

Moral of the Story

Sometimes, it is the challenges we fear the most that God uses to lift us up higher. Trust His strength, even when you feel like you are not strong enough.

Scripture Verse

"I can do all things through Christ who strengthens me." — Philippians 4:13

Reflection Questions

1. What "wind" is blowing in your life right now that feels too strong for you?

2. What may God be asking you to release and trust Him with in that situation?

3. When have you seen or felt strength or growth from a circumstance that you first thought was scary or impossible?

10
The Rock and The River
(Unshakeable Faith)

There was once a rock called Rami. Rami stood at the edge of a wide, rushing river. The river rushed and flowed past Rami for several years. Sometimes, it flowed gently; sometimes, it was angry and raging, but Rami was solid and unmoving. Rami was proud of his steadfastness. He believed that his strength and stillness would always keep him safe.

One spring, the rains fell hard, like never before. The river swelled, roared, and barreled over its banks, tossing branches and leaves in its wake. Many smaller rocks were washed downstream in just a few minutes! Even trees by the river's edge were groaning as the current pushed and tugged on their roots.

In that moment, Rami felt the river's water push against him with a force that it had never done before. For a split second, he felt a shiver. *Maybe I'm not as strong as I think, he thought to himself. Maybe this river will wash me away.*

But then, deep inside himself, Rami remembered something the old stones whispered so many years before: "Stand firm, and the river will flow around you."

So Rami anchored himself more firmly in the river bed. The water current slammed against him, swirling and churning, but he did not yield. He stood firm and allowed the river to wash over him without fear.

Hours passed. When the river finally calmed, Rami was still there, surrounded by other smaller stones that had been deposited nearby, forming a quiet little pool. The river had caused some change to the land, but it did not change or move Rami.

In that moment, Rami learned something powerful: unshakable faith is not about avoiding the storms of life; it is trusting than a strength greater than his could hold him firm and steady in life's turbulent waters.

Moral of the Story

Faith that rests in God is like a rock in rushing waters. The storms may come, but with the strength of God, we can stand still, firm, and unshaken.

Scripture Verse

"Be watchful, stand firm in the faith, be courageous, be strong." - 1 Corinthians 16:13 (WEB)

Reflection Questions

1. When has life felt like a rushing river that tested your faith?

2. What does "stand firm" in God's strength and trust mean to you?

3. How can you prepare your own heart to trust God in the next storm you might face?

11
The Clock with No Hands
(*Trusting in God's Perfect Timing*)

In a quaint, little workshop, there was a peculiar clock named Callen. Callen was different than all of the other clocks because Callen had no hands. The numbers were carefully painted on Callen's face, the gears gently ticked, but there wasn't anything to indicate what the time was.

Callen was anxious, every hour the other clocks chimed and their hands breezed across the face marking the hour of the day while Callen sat still. *"Why am I here if I can't tell time,"* he thought. *"What if I never know when the right time comes."*

A gentle old clockmaker noticed Callen's anxiousness. She picked him up, and said: "Callen, you do not need hands to know the right time. You just need to trust that things will happen when they are supposed to; your time will come."

Days passed and Callen sat, watching the other clocks chime and swing their hands, while Callen sat and waited. There were times when it was difficult not to feel forgotten. Sometimes it was hard not to feel like he would never serve a purpose.

Then one morning, the clock maker placed him on a pedestal at the center of town. The people gathered to watch with anticipation; they were waiting to hear a surprise announcement. And in that moment, Callen's inner gears began to move perfectly. A gentle chime rang loud and the people gasped with delight. Callen had marked the exact moment of celebration.

It was then that Callen realized that he had never been useless or forgotten, even without hands. He had simply been waiting on God's perfect timing, which, though unseen, is never late.

Moral of the Story
God's timing is perfect, even when it seems as if nothing is happening. Being patient and waiting is often part of the plan.

Scripture Verse
"He has made everything beautiful in its time..." - Ecclesiastes 3:11

Reflection Questions
1. Have you ever felt like you were waiting too long for something to happen? What did it feel like?
2. How can you trust God's will and timing rather than rushing ahead on your own?
3. What is one way you can patiently prepare your heart for what God is planning for you?

12

The Owl Who Asked Too Many Questions
(*Learning to Trust Without Full Understanding*)

Once upon a time, in a quiet portion of the forest, there lived an owl named Olive. Olive lived high up in a tall oak tree. Olive was wise – or at least she thought she was. Olive had one thing about her that was different from all the other animals, and it was that Olive asked questions. All. The. Time.

"Why does the sun go down?" she would ask the squirrels.

"Why does the river bend this way?" she would ask the deer.

"Why does the wind blow harder some days than others?" she would ask the fox.

The other forest animals were growing weary of Olive's endless questions. They would shake their heads saying, "Sometimes you just have to accept things as they are."

Olive did not want to accept "things" that she did not understand. One night, with the moon shining down and the stars twinkling like silver fire, she spotted a rabbit trapped in a tangle of vines. Olive wanted to help the rabbit but she hesitated.

How did this incident happen? Why could the rabbit not see the trap? Why was I not awake to warn him sooner? she whispered.

The wise old owl living in the next tree over moved closer. "Olive," he said kindly, "you do not have to know everything. Just trust that your instincts, courage, and God's guidance will be enough."

Olive hesitated, but then swooped down. Very carefully with her sharp talons, she pulled the vines off the rabbit. The rabbit hopped away free and thankful.

As Olive settled back on her branch she understood, she did not need to have all the answers in order to make the right choice. Sometimes, trusting God, and taking the next step forward, even when things are unclear, is the right choice.

Moral of the Story

We do not have to know everything in order to trust God. Sometimes, faith means that we act even when we do not have all the answers.

Scripture Verse

"Trust in the Lord with all your heart and lean not on your own understanding; in all your ways acknowledge Him, and He will direct your path." - Proverbs 3:5-6

Reflection Questions

1. Are there areas in your life that you feel the need to understand everything before taking action?

2. How can you begin to trust God even when you do not have all the answers?

3. Can you think of a time when moving forward in faith had a positive result – what did it feel like to trust before knowing the entire plan?

13
The Clay in the Potter's Hands
(Surrendering Control)

In a small, sunlit workshop sat a lump of clay on the table. Her name was Cora. She was soft, pliable, and had great potential. But she had one problem: she didn't want to be molded.

"What if I don't like what I turn out to be?" she thought. *"What if the potter makes me into something that I won't want to be?"*

The potter was a gentle old man. He smiled while picking her up and said, "Cora, trust me. I see what you can become."

Cora wriggled and swirmed. She resisted every push and pull. She wanted to stay the way she was—familiar and safe. But, the potter had steady hands. He pressed, stretched, and shaped

Cora. Sometimes, it felt uncomfortable, while at other times, it felt like she might just tear.

Days went by. The potter smoothed out her edges. He shaped her into something very pretty and useful. And finally, when he put her on the shelf to dry, Cora looked around and realized she was beautiful! More than she imagined. More than she could have done alone.

She realized something very important–letting go of control and surrendering to the one who knows the design brings a greater purpose than trying to stay in control.

Moral of the Story

When we allow God to shape our lives instead of being stuck in what we want, He can shape us into something much more beautiful and purposeful than we could even plan for ourselves.

Scripture Verse

"For we are His workmanship, created in Christ Jesus for good works, which God prepared beforehand that we should walk in them." — Ephesians 2:10

Reflection Questions

1. Are there places in your life where you are resisting God's shaping?

2. What fears stop you from surrendering to God?

3. How do you think your life would look if you fully trusted God to mold you according to His plan?

14

The Tree Who Lost Its Leaves
(Trust in Barren Seasons)

At the edge of a quiet forest, there was a tall oak tree named Tahlia. Every spring and summer, her branches were heavy with leaves, and birds made nests among them. But one autumn, a harsh storm swept through the forest and stripped Tahlia of all of her leaves.

At first, Tahlia felt empty. She looked at her bare branches and said, "What is the point of standing here if I have nothing to give?" The other trees, who were still holding onto a few stubborn leaves murmured, "It looks like your time is over."

Then, the winter came. The snow dusted Tahlia's bare branches, and she shivered in the cold, remembering the warmth of her leaves and the bright green color they used to be. But deep inside, she felt a quiet nudge: *Stand firm. Winter is not the end.*

As the days rolled by, she trusted the rhythm of the seasons, staying firmly planted with her roots in the soil, allowing her branches to sway in the wind and drop whatever they didn't need. She soaked up the sunlight and drank in the rain, even when it felt like nothing was happening to her.

Then came spring; tiny buds speckled her branches, and slowly leaves emerged! New leaves brighter and stronger than ever before. Thank God! She realized that while she couldn't see them, she had been growing all along and preparing for a transformation to a stronger, fuller life.

Moral of the story

Barren seasons are not wasted seasons; they are times of hidden growth. Trust God's timing, even when nothing seems to be happening.

Scripture Verse

"He shall be like a tree planted by the rivers of water, that brings forth its fruit in its season, whose leaf also shall not wither; and whatever he does shall prosper." - Psalm 1:3

Reflection Questions

1. Have you ever been in a season of emptiness or lack of productivity before? What did you do with that?
2. How can you trust God in the seasons that feel like nothing is happening?
3. What "roots" (faith, habits, relationships) can you develop during a barren season to prepare for growth?

15
The Moth and the Moonlight
(Chasing Temporary vs Eternal)

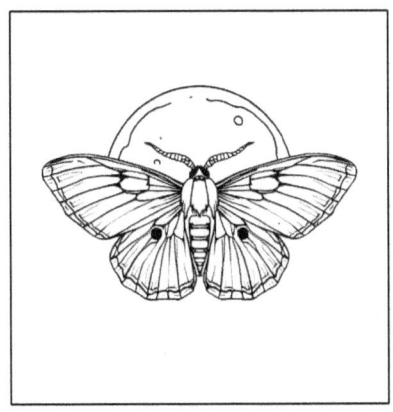

Once there was a little moth named Myra, who lived by a little meadow. Each night, the night sky would spill bright silver moonlight on the grass and Myra loved that glow. It felt so serene, almost alive–as if it whispered to her. Each night she would fly to that brilliant glow in the night.

Myra's mother, and all the other older moths would warn, "Myra, the moonlight is beautifully alluring, but it can never hold you. It is not real food, it is not real warmth. It cannot save you."

But Myra would never listen. She could not help herself. Night after night, she would fly to the glow, spiraling and circling it.

There were moments when she found herself too close to some trees or too close to the glowing lanterns the humans would set out, and she would feel fear in her wings. But the moonlight was so alluring.

Then one evening, she found herself exhausted, hovering near a bright lantern that glowed like the moon. The heat was strong and her wings singed. She soon realized that what seemed to her as beautiful and captivating from a distance could not sustain her.

A gentle voice drifted on the wind, it was her mother. "Myra, the glow is lovely, but don't forget what holds you when the glow fades—the steady things you've always had. Let the night be beautiful, but return to the quiet gifts that keep you, the ones that wait without fanfare and never fail."

Myra hovered weary and shaken; finally she turned from the foreign glow and back toward the safety of the meadow. There she found the sweetest nectar in the flowers, the comfort of soft grass, and the joy of being with other moths. The light she had chased was fleeting, but the blessings she had ignored were eternal.

Moral of The Story

While chasing the temporary pleasures of this world can lead to harm, trusting in God's eternal guidance leads to true, lasting fulfillment.

Scripture Verse

"Set your minds on things above, not on things on the earth."
— Colossians 3:2

Reflection Questions

1. What are the things in your life that appear to be the bright and enticing, but may not be good for you?

2. Instead of temporary distractions, how can you shift your focus onto God's eternal guidance?

3. What is one small step you could take today to "fly toward" what is lasting and true, rather than what only seems beautiful?

16
The Scared Shepherd Boy
(When God Calls the Unqualified)

Matheo was a small boy who watched over his father's sheep on a nice hillside. He was small and nervous and constantly doubted himself. He would watch the older shepherds who were very confident moving among the flock and guiding them into the pastures and wishing that he could also be as brave.

But, there was a problem. The shepherds were being overcharged by tax collectors and they did not know what to do about it.

One evening, while Matheo was counting the sheep, a voice said, "Matheo, go into the village and speak to the king."

Matheo froze in shock, "Me? I am just a shepherd boy, I don't know what to say. I am not brave enough. I am not important enough."

"Matheo," the voice said gently, "do not be afraid. I will be with you. I have chosen you."

Matheo's heart started to beat fast. The other shepherds would laugh at him if they saw him leave. The task was impossible. But very slowly, he began to figure out: he didn't have to be perfect, he just needed to trust God and take the first step.

The next morning, Matheo mustered up some courage, left the hillside and headed for the village. As Matheo walked to the village, God gave him the right words; by the time he faced the King he spoke with confidence. The king listened and acted, and the situation that seemed impossible was resolved!

Matheo walked back to his sheep in amazement. He learned something important that day. God often calls the unqualified, not to expose their weaknesses, but to display his strength through them.

Moral of the Story

God can use anyone, including those who feel small or unqualified, to do great things when they trust Him.

Scripture Verse

"But God chose the foolish things of the world to shame the wise; God chose the weak things of the world to shame the strong." — 1 Corinthians 1:27

Reflection Questions

1. Have you ever felt unqualified for something God called you do?

2. How might the trust in God help you to take steps that you feel too weak for?

3. What is one "small step" you can do today, even if it feels scary?

17
The Lost Trail and the Gentle Voice
(*Hearing and Following God's Whisper*)

In a thick, green forest, Liora, a young traveler, was lost and trying to find her way back home. She had been following a trail all morning. Now, the trail was twisted and unclear. The sun was setting behind the trees and behind the shadows of the trees, the forest looked bigger and scarier than it had before.

Suddenly, Liora's heart raced in her chest. She started calling for help, only to hear her own voice echo among the trees. She started to panic and thought, "*What if I never find my way? What if I am lost forever?*"

Just as Liora was about to give up in despair, she heard a still soft voice.

"Turn here Liora. Follow the small stones, not the obvious path."

The voice was quiet; almost easy to miss; but there was something about it that felt safe and wise. Liora hesitated. She wanted to find her original path, the one that she thought she knew. But she took a deep breath, trusted the whisper, and with slow steps began following the small stones, one careful step at a time.

Liora noticed the forest beginning to change. The trees were not as dense, the light was warmer, and she recognized some of the original landmarks that she had passed, just not to long ago. In a matter of minutes Liora was on a path she recognized; and it was headed home.

Liora now realized the gentle voice had guided her through the unknown. She only understood a part of the plan, but trusting the whisper led her exactly where she needed to go.

Moral of the Story

God's guidance can be calm and quiet. Learning to listen and follow His gentle direction will lead to safety in confusing and uncertain times.

Scripture Verse

"Your ears shall hear a word behind you, saying, 'This is the way, walk in it,' whenever you turn to the right hand or whenever you turn to the left." — Isaiah 30:21

Reflection Questions

1. Have you ever felt uncertain about which way to go, yet felt a small nudge from God?

2. How can you practice listening for that gentle whisper from God in your everyday living?

3. What is one small step you can take today to follow God's guidance, even if the path is unclear?

18
The Tethered Lamb
(Boundaries that Protect)

There was a little lamb named Lani. Lani lived in a beautiful, quiet meadow. She loved to explore and play in the soft grass, among the wildflowers and cool stream that curved through the field. But Lani's mother had a rule: a tether tied Lani to the safe post outside the barn.

At first, Lani didn't get it. "Why can't I roam free like the other lambs?" "Why do I have to stay so close?"

However, one morning the wind picked up, and a huge storm rolled into their meadow. The other lambs were having a great time chasing the leaves and other debris that the wind pushed around. Lani, who was tethered safely, watched closely.

Suddenly a loud crack came from the nearby trees and lightning flash through the sky. The wild wind raged on and caused the other lambs to panic. Scared and with nowhere safe to go, they ran around in circles.

But Lani was safe.

And this was when Lani started to realize that the tether that felt like a restriction was actually protection. Her mother's tether had kept her safe from the invisible danger of the storm.

When the storm passed, Lani was very thankful. She came to understand an important truth: boundaries aren't to hinder us — boundaries keep us safe until we are mature enough to handle more freedom wisely.

Moral of the Story
Boundaries protect and guide us. Learning to trust God's limits helps us stay safe and strong, even when we do not understand.

Scripture Verse
"There is a way that seems right to a man, But its end is the way of death." — Proverbs 14:12

Reflection Questions
1. Are there any boundaries/rules in your life that feel frustrating? How might they be protecting you?

2. How can you learn to trust God's guidance, even when it limits what you want to do?

3. What is one aspect of your life where following a boundary could keep you safe or help you grow?

19

The Pebble in the Sling
(God Uses the Small to Do Great Things)

In a small valley, a shepherd boy named David sat heartily tending his small flock of sheep. One day, as he tended his sheep, a giant named Goliath appeared challenging the villagers with his size and strength, and they all were terrified.

David was small, young, and inexperienced in battle. He wanted to take on the giant, but the villagers laughed at the thought of David going against Goliath. Saying, "you're just a boy, what can you do?"

David had something stronger than size, strength, or experience; he had trust in God who had helped him protect the sheep from dangers in the wild. David picked up five smooth pebbles from the brook and placed one in his sling.

As Goliath moved toward him, David threw back the sling, aimed, and released the stone. The pebble flew straight and true, hitting the giant in his forehead. Goliath fell to the ground and David took the giant's sword and slew him with it. Silence was in the valley for a few seconds, and then the villagers roared with shouts of amazement.

David encountered something powerful: God does not need our strength; even a small thing in our hands, when used with faith, can accomplish great things.

Moral of the Story
God can use even the smallest and seemingly weakest of us to accomplish mighty victories, when we trust in Him.

Scripture Verses
"For the battle is the Lord's, and He will give you into our hands." — 1 Samuel 17:47

"Not by might nor by power, but by My Spirit," says the Lord of hosts"— Zechariah 4:6

Reflection Questions
1. Have there been times you felt too small, or not qualified to make a difference?

2. How can you trust God to use your gifts, regardless of how small they may seem?

3. What "pebble" in your life, may God be able to use for a greater purpose?

20
The Bridge That Took Time to Build
(Faith in the Long Process)

Across a wide, rushing river was a village that was cut off from the neighboring town. People wanted to have a bridge that connected the two, but the river was fast and unpredictable. Many villagers tried to build a crossing quickly, but the strong current washed away their hard work.

There was a builder, a young woman named Leona, who did not give up. She worked patiently, placing stone upon stone, and taking time to shape each piece. The villagers laughed at her. "You're taking too long!" they said. "Why not rush it like the others?"

But Leona knew that the bridge could not be rushed. She studied the river's patterns, tested the foundations, and took time to revisit each stone, trusting it to remain strong, solid and consolidated. Days went by and turned into weeks, and weeks turned into months. Leona faced setbacks–floods, broken ropes, and slipping stones. Each time, she started again, learning, adjusting, and trusting.

Finally, after much time, effort and faith, the bridge was complete and stood strong. The villagers went on their first trip across the bridge. They were impressed with the strong structure that had been built with care, patience, and determination.

Leona smiled, knowing the journey was as important as the bridge itself. She understood that trusting the process, as well as God's timing, creates something that lasts.

Moral of the Story
Good things take time. And often, it takes faith, patience, and persistence to see results that last.

Scripture Verse
"Trust in the Lord with all your heart, and lean not on your ow understanding; in all your ways acknowledge Him, and He shall direct your paths." - Proverbs 3:5-6

Reflection Questions
1. Have you ever worked on something that took a lot of time to see result? How did you stay patient?
2. How can you trust in God's timing in the midst of long or difficult projects?
3. What is one small, steady step you can take today towards achieving a goal that feels distant?

21

The Spider's Broken Web
(Starting Over with God's Help)

In a secluded corner of a garden, there was a spider named Silvi, who had spent days weaving a beautiful, intricate web across the branches. The web glistened in the morning dew, perfect and strong, or so she thought!

One night, a storm rolled in, the wind howled, and the rain poured down. The next morning came, and Silvi's web was tattered into shreds. Every gossamer thread was gone! Silvi hung there – exhausted and heartbroken. "All that work....gone," she sighed in a low whisper, "where do I even start? This just feels hopeless."

Just then, a gentle breeze seemed to whisper through the leaves: *You are not alone. Start again.*

Silvi hesitated, but climbed slowly back to the starting point. She remembered when she was weaving the first web and all that she had learned: where to place the next strand, how to reinforce corners, and how to work carefully and patiently. So, step by step and thread by thread, Silvi began rebuilding her web.

It was not easy–not everything was perfect at first. Some strands sagged; some sections were not symmetrical. But she persisted and kept working. By morning, Silvi's web sparkled in the sunshine once again, but this time it was stronger than the first web. Silvi realized that when things fall apart, God provides the courage, wisdom, and strength to start over.

Moral of the Story

When life breaks our plan, with God's help we can begin again–stronger than before. Faith and persistence lead to restoration.

Scripture Verse

"The Lord is near to those who have a broken heart, and saves such as have a contrite spirit." — Psalm 34:18

Reflection Questions

1. Have you ever had something very important to you fall apart? How did you respond?
2. How can we trust God to help us start over when things are ruined?
3. What is one "web" in your life that God is working with you to rebuild today?

22

The Little Boat in the Big Storm
(Peace in God's Presence)

On a wide, choppy lake, a small boat named Bella was floating gently. Bella, carried a young boy named Jonas who loved to explore the lake and watch the sparkle of the water in the sunshine. One afternoon, dark clouds rolled in and a storm began to develop over the lake. The little boat tossed up and down in the waves and the wind howled causing Jonas to cling tightly to the sides of the boat in fear.

Bella felt small and fragile. "We can't fight this storm," Jonas whispered. "What if we tip over? What if we sink?"

Then suddenly, he remembered something his Grandmother told him, *"When the storm comes, trust God. He is with you in the boat."*

Jonas closed his eyes, took a deep breath, and spoke a quiet prayer asking God for courage and peace about the storm. In that moment, the storm did not disappear completely, however, Bella steadied. The wind still blew, the waves still heaved, yet the boy felt calm and safe because he knew that God was with him.

Slowly the storm passed. The lake settled into small ripples and the sun began to break through the clouds. Bella floated safely to shore. Jonas learned that even when the waves of life became fierce and threatening, God's presence brings peace that nothing else could provide.

Moral of the Story

When we face storms in life, trusting God and seeking His presence brings peace and protection.

Scripture Verse

"When you pass through the waters, I will be with you; and through the rivers, they shall not overflow you." — Isaiah 43:2

Reflection Questions

1. Have you encountered a situation in your life that felt like a storm? How did you respond?

2. How might remembering God's presence help you be calm in the storm?

3. What is one way you can invite God on your "boat" today, when life feels uncertain?

23
The Rooster Who Thought He Knew Best
(Humbling Pride)

Once upon a time, on a sunny farm, there was a proud rooster named Rolly. Rolly strutted around the farmyard each morning. He crowed grandly, convinced that he knew everything there was to know about the farm. He knew exactly when to wake the animals; he knew when it was meal time; he even knew where to find the best worms.

The other animals would roll their eyes and shake their heads in disbelief. "Rolly," they would say, "sometimes it is good to have a listening ear." But Rolly never listened; he thought he always knew best.

Then, one morning, a new farmer showed up, and the farmer had plans to rearrange the fields. Once again, Rolly scornfully ignored what was being asked of him and led the animals his way. They ran in circles, tripped on rocks, and ended up far from the safety of the barn.

Rolly was red in the face, flustered and disgraced. The animals looked around and sighed, realizing they were lost. Just then, the farmer gently called to them, reassuringly guiding them back safely.

No amount of crowing could save Rolly from his embarrassment. As he hung his face low, he realized that his pride had blinded him to the help and wisdom that was right in front of him. So, from that day onward, Rolly learned to listen first, crow second, and humbly accept directions. Rolly came to understand that pride leads to trouble; but, humility leads to safety and growth.

Moral of the Story
Pride can blind us from seeing the wisdom and guidance that is available to us. Humility, faith, and trust open our hearts to learn, grow and follow God's direction.

Scripture Verse
"Humble yourselves in the sight of the Lord and He will lift you up." — James 4:10

Reflection Questions
1. Have you ever acted as if you knew best and found out later that you were wrong?
2. How can humility help you make better choices in life?
3. What is one area you can practice listening before reacting to today?

24
The King's Letter
(Trusting the Word)

In a thriving kingdom, there was a messenger named Talia. Talia was entrusted with a very important letter from the king. In it was a message that contained instructions that could save the village from famine; but, the words seemed hard to understand and some villagers might question whether the letter was real.

Talia hesitated. "What do I do if they do not believe me? What if I make a mistake?" she wondered.

Then, she remembered what the king had said: *"Trust the message, and it will guide you."*

With great courage, Talia went to the village leaders to deliver the letter. She read the letter aloud. At first, the leaders were skeptical, but as they started following the instructions, food began to reach the village, they maintained full wells, and the villagers' hearts were filled with relief and gratitude.

Then, Talia realized something important: even when instructions are confusing or hard to believe, trusting the source and following the instructions faithfully brings life and provisions.

Moral of the Story

The Word of God is trustworthy. When we obey it, even if we don't fully understand it, it brings guidance, protection, and blessing.

Scripture Verse

"Your word is a lamp to my feet and a light to my path." — Psalm 119:105

Reflection Questions

1. Have you ever struggled to trust God, or His Word, or direction? What helped you?

2. How can you practice following God's leading faithfully, even when it feels confusing?

3. What is one verse or promise from the Bible that you can hold on to today?

25
The Quiet Field
(*Fruit Comes in Hidden Places*)

At the edge of a very busy orchard, there was a little, quiet field that had been forgotten by many. In this little field was a young apple tree named Eliora. Unlike the other trees in the orchard, Eliora was not planted in rows, and she did not have gardeners checking on her leaves or watering her everyday.

Sometimes, Eliora felt neglected. She watched the orchard trees grow and strong trees, with their branches heavy with fruit.

"*Will I ever produce anything*?" Eliora wondered.

The seasons came and went. The rains fell gently, urging Eliora's roots to drink. The sun warmed her leaves, and the wind helped her roots to grow deeper. Quietly, and slowly, without anyone noticing, Eliora's branches began to fruit–little sweet apples that were tastier than the orchard fruit.

Eventually, a few travelers walked through the little field and were amazed. "How could this little tree in the quiet field have fruit with delicious taste?" they asked. Eliora smiled quietly to herself. Eliora learned to trust the slow, hidden process of growth, knowing that God's care was constant, even when she could not see it.

Moral of the Story

Growth and fruitfulness often happen quietly. Trust God in seasons that seem hidden, He is at work even when we can't see it.

Scripture Verse

"But the fruit of the Spirit is love, joy, peace, longsuffering, kindness, goodness, faithfulness, gentleness, self-control." Galatians 5:22-23

Reflection Questions

1. Have you ever felt overlooked or unrecognized while others appeared to be flourishing?

2. How do you trust God to work quietly in your life, when you do not see the results right away?

3. What is one small way you can walk with patience and faith during hidden seasons of growth?

26

The Firefly Who Wanted to Shine Like the Stars
(Comparison and Trust)

One quiet night in the meadow, little Farah was among the fireflies, singing softly, and letting their music flow through the sky. Farah flickered softly and shined a small light, only slightly bigger than a pinpoint. She liked her glow, but when she looked above her to the sky, the stars were much brighter, and their shine seemed so perfect.

"I wished I could shine like that," said Farah, with a full sigh. "My light is too small, it doesn't matter."

Nearby, an older firefly named Orion was listening. "Farah," he said with compassionate energy, "your light does not have to be like the light of the stars. You have your own place, your own glow, and someone out there needs your light."

Farah thought for a second. Could her small flickering light really matter in this huge world? Later that night, a beetle that was lost wandered into the meadow. It was very dark and cold and the beetle could not find its way. And then, Farah lit up, guiding the beetle to a safe spot on the soft grass where it could rest.

For the first time, Farah discovered though she had a small light, but it made a big difference. She didn't need to compare herself to the stars, she just needed to glow where she was.

Moral of the Story

Comparison steals joy. Trust that God has given you your own light and purpose, and that every small difference matters.

Scripture Verse

"You are the light of the world. A city that is set on a hill cannot be hid." — Matthew 5:14

Reflection Questions

1. Do you ever compare yourself to people around you and feel like your gifts are too small?

2. In what ways can you focus on using your own "light" to help or encourage someone today?

3. What is one unique gift or talent that you can trust God to use for good, right where you are?

27

The Shepherd's Map
(God's Guidance is Never Late)

Micah was a young shepherd who had been tending his flock of sheep for several months. One day, he had to lead the sheep to a new pasture across a large unknown valley. Micah was anxious; he did not know the safest way, or was concerned about cliffs, streams and wild animals.

As Micah wonderd what to do, his grandfather arrived from the village and gave him an old map that he had used before. "Micah, just follow this map! Trust the directions. It will lead you and the sheep safely."

Micah took the map and examined it, still unsure. "But this seems really hard..." he thought to himself. "The path on the map feels longer than I thought it would be, and it has some marks on it I don't understand."

Nonetheless, Micah followed what his grandfather told him. He took the sheep along the winding paths, over the hills, and across the streams. Along the way, Micah stumbled and worried, but each time the map led him safely in the right direction for the flock. What had seemed uncertain at first turned out to be exactly what the flock needed.

By the time they arrived in the new pasture, Micah came to an important realization: even when it seems late or confusing, God's guidance arrives at the perfect moment, bringing safety and provision.

Moral of The Story

Trust that God's guidance is always on time. Trust Him, even when the path seems uncertain or delayed.

Scripture Verse

"Your word is a lamp to my feet and a light to my path." - Psalm 119:105

Reflection Questions

1. Do you remember a time you felt lost and wished you had waited for God's guidance?
2. How can you trust God's timing, even when directions seem unclear?
3. What step you can take today to follow His direction?
4. How can you treat God's Word like a map—trusting its directions even when the path feels uncertain?

28
The Wind and the Wheat
(Learning to Bend in Surrender)

In a golden field of wheat were tall stalks of wheat swaying proudly in the sunshine. Each day, as the wind would blow across the field, Willa and some of the other stalks would gently sway. Some days the wind was a gentle breeze; some days the wind was fierce. Most of the stalks, however, resisted and fought the wind, standing rigid and stiff. But one day, it was really windy, and as the wind blew, some stalks snapped and fell to the ground.

Willa experienced the wind like most of the other stalks. But Willa had learned to bend with the wind instead of resisting the wind. Initially, Willa thought that resisting was better because resisting looked like strength, but as the wind blew much more, she realized that bending with the wind does not mean weakness or giving up; it meant trusting the wind to safely guide her.

As the seasons passed and harvest finally came, all of the wheat stalks who bent with the wind stood ready – proud and tall and golden. The stalks that resisted the winds and fought the winds were broken and ruined. Willa learned something very important: through humility and surrender when the forces were beyond her control, she was able to grow stronger, taller and more fruitful.

Moral of the Story

Flexibility and surrendering to God's will helps to withstand life's challenges. Trusting God allows us to grow stronger instead of breaking under pressure.

Scripture Verse

"Blessed is the man who trusts in the Lord, and whose hope is the Lord." - Jeremiah 17:7

Reflection Questions

1. Are there areas of life you have struggled in due to resisting God's guidance?

2. How can you learn to bend in surrender instead of break under pressure?

3. What is the one situation today where you can trust God and allow Him to lead?

29

The Vine That Stayed Connected
(Trust Through Abiding)

In a bright, sunlit vineyard, the young vine, Violette, looked to her surroundings and stretched out her tendrils towards the warm light from the sun. Violette admired the other vines that were next to her that seemed to grow really quickly and produce fruit. Immediately, Violette thought of the old gardener's words, *"Stay connected to the roots. That is the source of your strength."*

At first, Violette began to feel impatient. "Why is it that I am growing slowly while all of the other vines are flourishing," she thought. Nevertheless, she hung on to the main vine, the lifeline that provided water, nutrients, and stability.

Over the course of seasons, the fast-growing vines eventually wilted in the heat or struggled in the storms. But, Violette remained healthy and strong because she was connected to the roots. When the fruiting time came, Violette's branches were heavy with plump, sweet grapes.

What Violette realized was that growth and fruitfulness doesn't come from rushing or trying to go it alone. Staying connected to the source of life provides strength, resilience, and fruitfulness that lasts.

Moral of the Story

Abiding in the Lord provides strength and nourishment. Trusting God and staying connected leads to the true growth and fruitfulness.

Scripture Verse

"I am the vine, you are the branches. He who abides in Me, and I in him, bears much fruit; for without Me you can do nothing."— John 15:5

Reflection Questions

1. Are there times when you attempted to do everything on your own instead of staying connected to the Lord?

2. How can you remain "abiding" with the Lord when life is busy or challenging?

3. In what way can you draw closer to the Lord today for strength, and direction?

30

The Key That Fit the Door
(Purpose and Divine Timing)

In a peaceful little village, there lived a young boy named Noa. Noa loved to explore things. One day, he found an old door with a lock on it at the edge of the town square. Noa was curious and experimented by trying to put every kind of key he had ever seen or thought of in the lock. He tried small keys, big keys, shiny keys, and old keys and couldn't find a key that opened this door.

Noa was frustrated with the lack of success and was ready to give up when an elder approached him and said "Sometimes, the right key comes at the right time; you just have to be patient and trust that God knows the perfect moment." Noa nodded, and though he didn't really understand, he decided to wait.

Days turned into weeks, and Noa was still waiting. He continued to explore the village, help his neighbors, and learn from the elders. One morning, while Noa was cleaning, he came across a simple, worn key in a forgotten corner of his house. Noa found the old key strange and thought he would try it on the old door at the town square. Noa walked back to the old door, put the key into the lock, and it fit perfectly. The door opened and inside the door was a treasure room, full of tools, craft ideas, seeds, and books that could help the entire village flourish!

Noa realized that God took him along a process so that he could grow and learn as he waited patiently. The key had been there all along, but Noa wasn't ready for the door until the right moment. Noa learned that his purpose and blessing came in God's divine timing, not his own.

Moral of the Story
God's timing is perfect. Your purpose will be revealed at the right moment–trust God's timing and grow while you wait.

Scripture Verse
"Many are the plans in a man's heart, but it is the Lord's purpose that will prevail." - Proverbs 19:21

Reflection Questions
1. Have you grown impatient as you wait for God to open a door of your life?
2. How can you trust God's timing when results are not immediate?
3. What is one thing you can do today to prepare for the purpose that God is shaping you for?

Conclusion

As we reach the end of these fables, one truth is evident: faith in God transforms how we deal with the challenges of life. The sparrows, ants, and fireflies we met all teach one fundamental lesson: when we trust God, even the smallest acts of faith can have remarkable results.

Remember, trust is a journey, not a single event. The journey can sometimes seem long, the wind may feel strong, or the outcomes may be unknown. But, God's presence is constant, and His plans are always good. Encourage children to practice faith in small actions of trust, and over time, those lessons will grow into a legacy of trust, courage, and hope.

May these fables encourage you to trust in, obey, and follow God. May the seeds of faith planted today grow into a lifetime of fruitfulness for your children, and generations after them.

Closing Prayer

Loving God, we give thanks for shaping our hearts and teaching us to trust You. Help us and our children to remember Your timing is perfect, Your plans are good, and Your love is unchanging. Grant us courage to face life's storms, patience in waiting, and faith to trust You in all things. May these stories encourage hearts to seek You, follow You, and dwell in Your peace. In Jesus name. Amen.

Resources for Your Family

For Printable Family Declarations & other resources, go to whollybooks.com

Other books by the author and contact

Other books by the author include:

1. Intentional Spiritual Parenting
2. Declarations to Speak Life Over Your Children — Nurturing Identity, Purpose, and Wisdom Through God's Word
3. Declarations to Speak Life Over Your Children — Nurturing Wellness, Courage, and Character Through God's Word
4. Declarations to Speak Life Over Your Children — Nurturing Leadership Impact and Authority in the Seven Mountains of Influence Through God's Word
5. Kingdom Lessons for Life: Christian Fables on Faith and Trust
6. Kingdom Lessons for Life: Christian Fables on Courage and Strength
7. Kingdom Lessons for Life: Christian Fables on Humility and Pride
8. Kingdom Lessons for Life: Christian Fables on Kindness and Compassion

Go to whollybooks.com for more information on books by the author. You can find our books at all your favorite bookstores and online retailers.

About the Author

Christy Ojikutu is a passionate advocate for raising children with strong faith and Kingdom values. Through her writing, she inspires families to nurture spiritual growth, resilience, and trust in God from a young age. Christy's work blends creativity, Scripture, and practical life lessons to help children see God's hand in everyday life and grow into confident, faith-filled adults.

Thank You

Thank you for choosing to journey through this book with me. Each story was written with the hope of planting seeds of faith, courage, and wisdom in the hearts of children and families. It means so much to know that these lessons will be shared in homes, classrooms, and bedtime moments where values are shaped and character is built.

With heartfelt gratitude for your dedication to raising children who reflect God's love and truth. May these fables be a gentle companion on your family's journey, sparking meaningful conversations, inspiring faith-filled choices, and planting seeds of wisdom that flourish for generations.